nickelodeon™

TEENAGE MUTANT NINJA TURTLES™

ROBOT RAMPAGE!

THIS BOOK BELONGS TO

your name here!

3 of my *favorite* books

① ....

② ....

③ ....

Here is a picture of **me**
after I finish a **great** book!

Dear Parent:

Congratulations! Your child is taking the first steps on an exciting journey. The destination? Independent reading!

STEP INTO READING® will help your child get there. The program offers five steps to reading success. Each step includes fun stories and colorful art. There are also Step into Reading Sticker Books, Step into Reading Math Readers, Step into Reading Phonics Readers, Step into Reading Write-In Readers, and Step into Reading Phonics Boxed Sets—a complete literacy program with something for every child.

Learning to Read, Step by Step!

Ready to Read   Preschool–Kindergarten
• big type and easy words • rhyme and rhythm • picture clues
For children who know the alphabet and are eager to begin reading.

Reading with Help   Preschool–Grade 1
• basic vocabulary • short sentences • simple stories
For children who recognize familiar words and sound out new words with help.

Reading on Your Own   Grades 1–3
• engaging characters • easy-to-follow plots • popular topics
For children who are ready to read on their own.

Reading Paragraphs   Grades 2–3
• challenging vocabulary • short paragraphs • exciting stories
For newly independent readers who read simple sentences with confidence.

Ready for Chapters   Grades 2–4
• chapters • longer paragraphs • full-color art
For children who want to take the plunge into chapter books but still like colorful pictures.

STEP INTO READING® is designed to give every child a successful reading experience. The grade levels are only guides. Children can progress through the steps at their own speed, developing confidence in their reading, no matter what their grade.

Remember, a lifetime love of reading starts with a single step!

Visit us on the Web!
StepIntoReading.com
randomhouse.com/kids

Educators and librarians, for a variety of teaching tools, visit us at RHTeachersLibrarians.com

ISBN 978-0-307-98212-4 (trade) – ISBN 978-0-307-98213-1 (lib. bdg.)

Printed in the United States of America   20 19 18 17 16 15 14 13 12 11

nickelodeon
TEENAGE MUTANT NINJA TURTLES

ROBOT RAMPAGE!

Adapted by Christy Webster

Illustrated by Patrick Spaziante

Based on the teleplay "Metalhead" by Tom Alvarado

Random House 🏠 New York

It was late at night. The Teenage Mutant Ninja Turtles were in an abandoned warehouse, battling their enemies, the Kraang. Inside each robot body was a blobby pink brain!

Smash! Raphael knocked out a Kraang.
A pink blob jumped out and scurried away.

Slam! Donatello tried to use his wooden
bo staff against another robot. It bounced
off. The robot was not hurt.

"Are you kidding me?" Donatello cried.

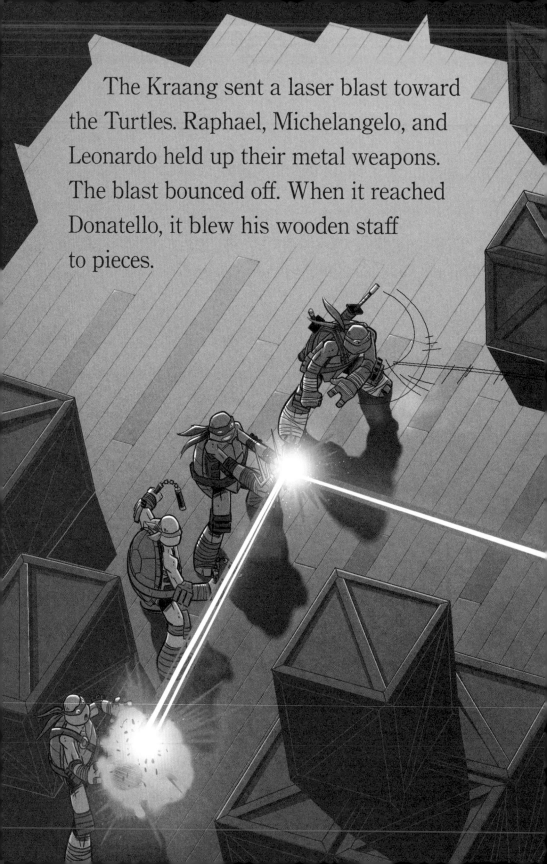

The Kraang sent a laser blast toward
the Turtles. Raphael, Michelangelo, and
Leonardo held up their metal weapons.
The blast bounced off. When it reached
Donatello, it blew his wooden staff
to pieces.

"Dude, your weapon just exploded!" Michelangelo said.

"Donnie, take cover!" Leonardo ordered.

The Kraang kept attacking. Leonardo threw a ninja star at a forklift and sent it plowing into the robots. The Turtles were safe.

Donatello found an empty Kraang robot. "Hey, guys, give me a hand with this," he said.

"What's it for?" Raphael asked.

"Don't you want to understand how these things work?" Donatello replied. The other Turtles helped him carry the robot back to their underground lair.

When they got there, they found their new friend April working on her computer. The Kraang had kidnapped April's dad, and the Turtles were trying to help her find him.

The Turtles' sensei, Splinter, walked into the room holding a new wooden staff. He handed it to Donatello.

"Look, Donnie's got another stick to break," Raphael taunted.

"I can't keep fighting with this," Donatello told Splinter. "I want to use modern technology."

"You may upgrade your weapon,"
Splinter said. "But remember, combat is
not a video game."

Donatello thought for a moment.
"That's it! I'll turn combat into a video
game!" he said. Splinter shook his head
while Donatello dragged the robot into
his lab.

"He's the smart one, right?" April
asked with a smirk.

The next day, April told Raphael and Leonardo about the website she had made. "It's a message board where people can post strange things they see around the city," she said. "It could help us find my dad."

Someone had posted a news video about a gas explosion in the warehouse district. April hit Pause. They could see a Kraang in the background!

"We'll check it out tonight," Leonardo said. "We can't go out in the daytime." Splinter didn't want people to see the Turtles.

"Well, I can," April said, and left the lair.

rehouse
plosion

April looked for the Kraang. She spotted one and followed it into a warehouse. She hid behind some barrels. She heard two robots talking about an experiment. They had a weird way of speaking, with words in the wrong order.

"The mutagen will be tomorrow unleashing in the water supply that supplies the humans' supply of water," one said. Mutagen was the radioactive ooze that had turned the Turtles into mutants. If the robots put it in the water, many people would mutate!

April gasped and turned to leave. She had to tell the Turtles! She knocked over a crate. The Kraang heard her! She kicked out the window, just like a ninja.

Back at the lair, Donatello was ready to reveal his new weapon. The other Turtles heard loud footsteps. *Boom! Boom! Boom!* They turned around and saw a robot that looked like a Turtle!

"Take me to your leader!" the robot
said in Donatello's voice. Donatello stepped
into the room holding a video game
controller. "Gentlemen, this is the future!"
he said.

"I always thought the future would be
taller," Raphael said.

"Isn't it cool?" Donatello said. "I built it from the Kraang parts. It can do all the dangerous stuff while we stay safe."

"So it's for wimps," Raphael said.

"Try it," Donatello said. "Attack."

Raphael, Leonardo, and Michelangelo all sparred with the new robot. But none of their attacks could make a dent.

"Let's call it Metalhead!" said Mikey.

That night, Michelangelo, Raphael, and Leonardo went out into the city. They leaped across rooftops and waited on a ledge.

Clang! Clang! Clang! Metalhead slowly caught up with them. Donatello was back in the lair, controlling the robot like a video game.

"Quiet!" Leonardo said. "Someone's coming!"

It was April. She gasped when she saw
Metalhead. "What is *that*?"
The Turtles explained about
Donatello's robot.
"We have to do something," April said.
"The Kraang are going to poison the city's
water supply with mutagen!"
April led the Turtles to the
Kraang's warehouse.

The Turtles got ready to confront the Kraang. Leonardo stepped in front of Metalhead.

"Donnie, I need you to hang back," he said. "Metalhead is too clumsy."

Clumsy!" Donatello said. Metalhead's
arms rose and punched a hole in the wall.
    "You're not coming, Donnie,"
Leonardo said.

Leonardo, Michelangelo, and Raphael sneaked up on the Kraang while April and Metalhead waited behind.

The Turtles lurked in the dark, watching the robots load mutagen onto trucks. Suddenly, they attacked! "Hi-yah!" Raphael shouted.

Metalhead waited with April on the rooftop. Back at the lair, Donatello could see April through the robot's eyes.

"She's so beautiful," Donatello said. "Good thing she can't tell I'm staring at her through the monitor."

Donatello's voice came out of the robot. April looked at it. "You know I can hear you, right?" she said.

Donatello laughed nervously. "Of course! I was just joking," he said. He pushed a button on the controller. "I hope she bought that," he said to himself. This time, the voice coming out of the robot was even louder!

"That's the megaphone," April said.

Donatello tried to change the subject.
"So, how do you think the guys are doing?"
he asked.

Just then, an energy blast shot through
the roof.

"They're everywhere!" Michelangelo
shouted. "Run!"
"Not good," said April.
It sounded like the three Turtles had
been cornered by the Kraang.

Suddenly, Metalhead crashed through the ceiling and landed in the middle of the action. The Turtles and the Kraang all stared.

"Why are you standing like that?" Leonardo asked. Metalhead's arms were in a weird position.

"Don't I look heroic?" Metalhead said in Donatello's voice.

"No!" Leonardo shouted.

"Sorry," the robot said, putting his hands on his hips. "Wrong button."

The battle with the Kraang continued. Metalhead really did seem invincible! The Kraang's lasers couldn't hurt him. The Turtles were finally winning!

Donatello watched from the lair, excited. He moved faster, blasting lasers all over the place. Finally, he found his target. *Boom!* The mutagen exploded.

The city's water supply was safe, but Metalhead was damaged in the explosion. Donatello lost contact with the robot. He was frantic. He pushed every button.

"Guys, if you can hear me, run!" he shouted.

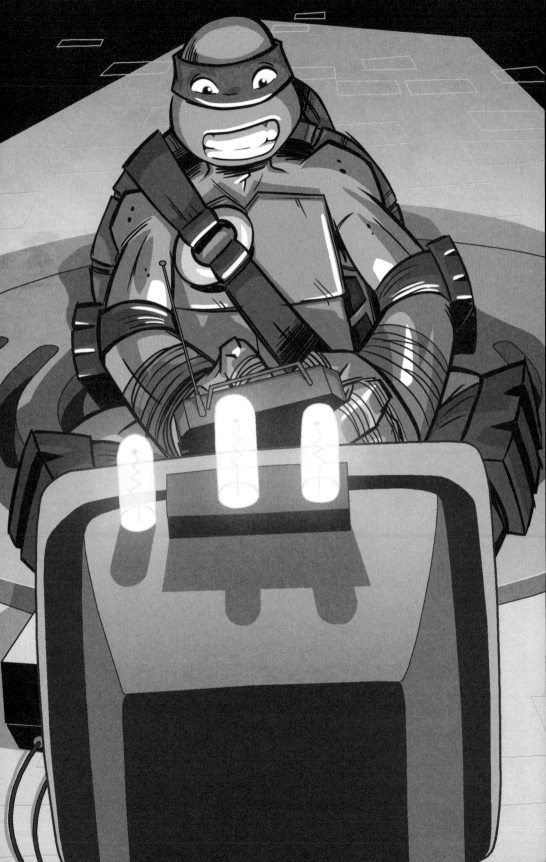

One Kraang blob jumped out of
its damaged robot and into Metalhead.
Metalhead's eyes glowed red. Now
the Kraang was controlling him! Evil
Metalhead attacked the Turtles.

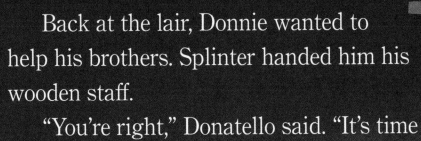

Back at the lair, Donnie wanted to help his brothers. Splinter handed him his wooden staff.

"You're right," Donatello said. "It's time to stop playing games." He ran out of the lair.

SYSTEM MONITOR

METALHEAD STATUS

0010101000010101010

0101010010101111010
1111110101010101010
1010100000000101010

0101010010101111010
1111110101010101010
1010100000000101010

ERRO

142526376
901285982
3982 8349
42728729
2223 8292
198151
71001760
82976482

When Donatello reached the warehouse, he faced off against Evil Metalhead. The other Turtles took on the Kraang. Donnie dodged attack after attack, until one blast broke his staff in half.

"Not again!" he shouted. He spotted a loose beam on the ceiling and positioned himself under it. "Come get me!" he called out to Evil Metalhead.

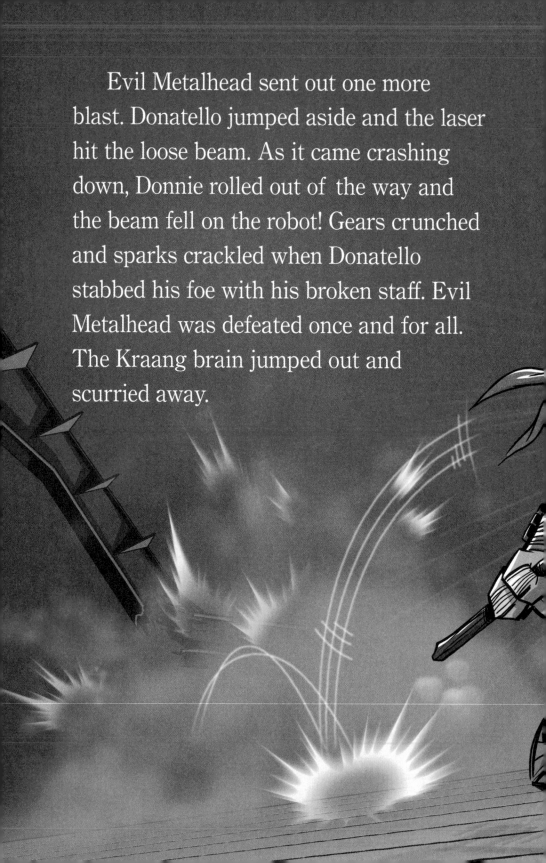

Evil Metalhead sent out one more blast. Donatello jumped aside and the laser hit the loose beam. As it came crashing down, Donnie rolled out of the way and the beam fell on the robot! Gears crunched and sparks crackled when Donatello stabbed his foe with his broken staff. Evil Metalhead was defeated once and for all. The Kraang brain jumped out and scurried away.

"Awesome!" Donatello shouted.
After defeating the last few Kraang,
Michelangelo and Leonardo patted
Donnie's back.

"Nice job, bro!" Mikey said. Donatello
was proud of himself.

"Not bad," Raphael said. "Except for
the part where you got us into this mess in
the first place."

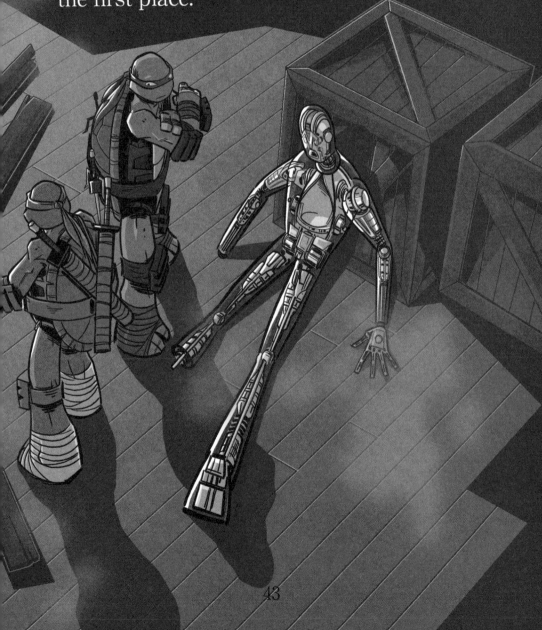

Back in the lair, Donatello began to work on a new project. Splinter thought he looked sad.

"What troubles you?" he asked.

"This was all my fault," Donatello said.

"Yes, you are responsible," Splinter replied. "But you are also responsible for saving the city."

Donatello felt better.

"In the end, there was nothing better than a wooden stick," he said. "Except a laser-guided wooden stick!"

Donatello held up the weapon he was working on. Then he slammed it against the ground. The staff started making a strange sound.

"It's not supposed to do that!"
Donatello cried. "Run!"